THE CAT
WITH THE COLOURED TAIL

THE CAT WITH THE COLOURED TAIL

Gillian Mears

Illustrated by
Dinalie Dabarera

WALKER BOOKS
AND SUBSIDIARIES

LONDON • BOSTON • SYDNEY • AUCKLAND

First published in 2015
by Walker Books Australia Pty Ltd
Locked Bag 22, Newtown
NSW 2042 Australia
www.walkerbooks.com.au

The moral rights of the author and illustrator have been asserted.

National Library of Australia Cataloguing-in-Publication entry:
Mears, Gillian, author.
The cat with the coloured tail / Gillian Mears; Illustrator, Dinalie Dabarera.
ISBN: 978 1 922077 40 0 (hardback)
For primary school age.
Subjects: Cats – Juvenile fiction.
Ice cream trucks – Juvenile fiction.
Ice cream cones – Juvenile fiction.
Color – Juvenile fiction.
Other Creators/Contributors: Dabarera, Dinalie, illustrator.
A823.3

The illustrations for this book were created with pencil
Typeset in Bernhard Modern
Printed and bound in China

For my sisters
Yvonne, Karin and Sonya.
Dog girls who have learned to love cats. GM

For all the cats who look at this book
and see a bed. DD

MR HOOPER'S ICE-CREAM TRUCK was not like any other ever seen. It was so round that if it pulled into a street on dusk, children thought, Oh, here comes the full moon. On wheels as small as silver buttons.

"Moon-creams" read the sign on the truck. "Your favourites guaranteed".

Ting-ting! rang the ice-cream bell. The Cat with the Coloured Tail loved the happy sound so much that he often gave the bell a ring too. *Ting-a-ting-TING!*

Mr Hooper's cat was not like any
ordinary cat. For a start, his face was the
shape of a heart. Most amazing of all, and
unlike any other cat in the world,
Mr Hooper's cat had a tail that could
change colour.

Most of the time, his long tail was the
colour of the rest of his coat, as silvery blue
as a bright new nail. His tail would only ever
change colour to help people feel happy.

The Cat with the Coloured Tail had first
come to Mr Hooper's truck as a silver kitten.
That was back when Mr Hooper was so lonely
even his ice-creams had looked sad (and not
many people had wanted to buy one).

What a small kitten The Cat with the
Coloured Tail had been. Appearing from
nowhere. With his little tail stuck straight up
in the air, quivering. Then how that tail had

quivered even faster, changing colour to
Mr Hooper's favourite colour combination –
red and yellow.

From that day on, The Cat with the
Coloured Tail and Mr Hooper were never
apart. Together, they'd invented moon-creams.
Together, they'd realised that the world was
full of the shape of hearts. Together, spotting
hearts was the game they loved to play.

After years of sharing his life with the cat,
Mr Hooper knew that hearts could be found
just about everywhere. Softly, he began to sing
one of his cat's songs.

Hearts on footpaths, hearts in leaves.
Hearts in certain apple seeds.
Hearts in trees, in scabs on knees.
Heart-shaped whispers on the breeze.

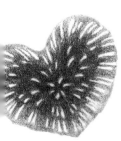

13

Today, Mr Hooper was not having much luck. Today, The Cat with the Coloured Tail had seen so many more hearts than Mr Hooper that he'd decided to give Mr Hooper a chance. He sauntered right past an ants' nest a couple of times. Closer and even closer.

After a while though, the cat felt like going crazy. It was so obvious. Couldn't Mr Hooper see what was right in front of his nose? That some ants had made their nest into the shape of a heart?

With a little miaow of affection, the cat almost touched the heart with the tip of his tail.

"Well, how did I miss that one?" asked Mr Hooper, shaking his head. "Whatever would I do without you?"

Now that Mr Hooper had finally seen the ants' nest built in the shape of a heart, the pleasant mood of the day deepened.

Mr Hooper scratched the bottom of The Cat with the Coloured Tail's ears in just the way his cat loved.

Pretending that he was still a kitten, The Cat with the Coloured Tail chased the tip of his tail. Mr Hooper always said that he was chasing the tail of happiness. Mr Hooper said that it looked like so much fun that he wished he had a tail.

Because he didn't, he did the next best thing. Out of his pocket, he drew a twig onto which he'd sewn a tiny red flag underneath a tiny yellow one. He put this into the ground next to the ants' home. Not only were red and yellow still Mr Hooper's favourite colours, but the twig would help other people notice the heart.

"Aren't we going well today?" Mr Hooper commented. "That's six hearts for you. One for me. But only because you helped me out."

Now his cat was staring up into the sky in a way that Mr Hooper knew could mean only one thing. Sure enough, there was a large blue heart carved out of clouds in the sky.

In the sun, The Cat with the Coloured Tail's coat shimmered like moonlight over water. He also seemed to have a slight smile on his face.

"A heart in the sky," said Mr Hooper happily. "You just have the knack. Seven for you it is. What can I get you for morning tea before we get back to work?" The cat was still looking at the heart made of sky and clouds. He didn't feel hungry. "Not even a triangle of my sardine sandwich?"

No. I don't want one, signalled the cat, turning away.

It wasn't like The Cat with the Coloured Tail to turn down a snack. What could be wrong?

The cat began to lick his paw and clean his face. There was an odd tingling sensation in his whiskers that usually meant his tail was changing, but when he turned to look, it was the same colour as the rest of his coat. Just for a moment though, an image of a darker heart, lonely and landlocked, had swum into the cat's mind. To dispel the thought, he half pounced at a cricket hopping by.

"Well, let's get going then," said Mr Hooper. Tomorrow their holidays were beginning, so there wasn't a moment to lose. He opened his truck's door and in jumped the cat. *Ting-ting!* Mr Hooper gave a few rings of the bell and tooted the horn.

Moon-creams, sang The Cat with the Coloured Tail. As always, only Mr Hooper heard the words.

Flowers were falling onto the road from trees. There was the feeling that it might storm later.

Every flavour of your dreams. Ting-a-ting-ting!

M R HOOPER NEVER FOLLOWED a set route
for selling their moon-creams. There was
never any need. When his cat's tail pointed left,
he turned the truck left. When the tail pointed
right, right would go the moon-shaped truck
on its button wheels.

When the cat's tail pointed straight up, it
was Mr Hooper's signal that somewhere very
close by was someone sad enough to be given a
moon-cream for free. If he lay in Mr Hooper's
lap with his tail curled, and yawned, that was

always the sign that it was time for a sleep,
maybe followed by more heart spotting if they
felt like it.

Moon-creams so dreamy,
All silvery blue,
sang The Cat with the Coloured Tail.

Moon-creams so dreamy,
All rosy and pink,
Try one for free and see sorrows sink.

Mr Hooper smiled to see his cat setting
out in the direction of the funniest, oldest
house in the street. There had never been a
sad person's home that his cat hadn't found
his way inside. Sure enough, after leaping an
impossibly high distance, in slipped his cat
through a half-open window.

Once inside, The Cat with the Coloured
Tail paused. So attuned were his ears that,
although the crying was soft, he could hear it
straightaway. Quietly, he made his way to
a bedroom door.

Oh, it was very sad. His whiskers turned
down at the sight. There on the bed, under
a rug, an old lady wasn't just asleep. She was
asleep crying. Something had made her so
unhappy that, even though her sleep had been
deep, her tears hadn't stopped falling.

Moon-creams so dreamy.
Puddings so creamy, sang the cat softly
and jumped up on the bed.

Then lick, lick, lick, lick, lick, he set to work
to dry her tears away.

Moon-creams so dreamy, he kept humming.

Now that there was no chance of getting
soaked by tears, he nestled into the crook of
her arm. Then he began to purr.

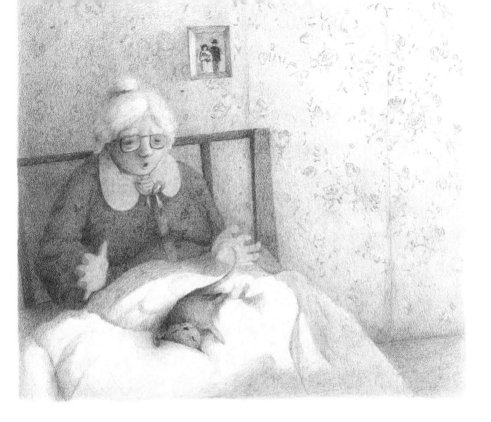

Just a little purr at first but getting louder
until he sounded like a warm engine chugging
in time with the beat of the old lady's heart.

At that moment, the old lady woke up.

"Goodness. If it isn't the tiniest grey cat I've
ever seen. But with the most loving purr. And,
am I dreaming, a pink tail?"

Without needing to ask, the cat just knew that pink was her most favourite colour of all. Not a lurid pink, not pink like a lollipop, but soft, like a fragrant old fashioned rose. Or the colour of an old lady's cheeks when a tiny cat has licked up all her tears.

"Wait. Little kitty. Please don't go."

For The Cat with the Coloured Tail had left the bed, pink tail high in the air, and was about to disappear out the door. But now he stopped, looking back at her as if to say, *Come on!*

Seeing that the cat's face was the shape of a heart had made the old lady think of love. And his colour was just that of her lovely fat childhood cat of long ago. Not that Old Grey's tail had ever turned pink.

Keeping just ahead, his soft pink tail straight up high, the cat led her out of the house.

Mr Hooper, on the lookout, seeing his

cat's tail, immediately set to work to make a
moon-cream of that exact colour. He made
it so that the middle was dark crimson for a
surprise, but the outside almost silver, like an
ordinary moon-cream, with just the faintest
blush of pink as a hint.

"But I'm afraid that I'm still in my
dressing-gown. With no
money anyway for that
lovely ice-cream."
The old lady
looked sad in the
way she must
have looked sad
when she was a
child.

"Ah," said
Mr Hooper.

"But these are moon-creams. Not always for sale. Especially pink ones."

Moon-creams, sang the cat,
Moon-creams so dreamy,
All pink and rosy.
Will make you feel happy,
Cat-licked and cosy.

"I made this one specially for you,"
Mr Hooper said to the old lady, handing across
an ice-cream that was like no other.

Because old ladies love ice-cream as much
as when they were tiny girls, Mr Hooper and
The Cat with the Coloured Tail couldn't help
smiling as they watched the old lady taking her
first lick. She thought that it tasted sublime,
as if it had been made of moonbeams and joy.
Under her tongue, it was delicious and cool.

Each sweet lick that the old lady took put more and more life into her walk, until she was skipping home, even as she licked.

To eat a moon-cream was like licking love and happiness both at once. After a moon-cream, life would always be luckier.

Extremely pleased, Mr Hooper sat back at the steering wheel. "She'll remember that, won't she, for the rest of her life?"

Thyyy dreams! Moon creams! sang the cat, sitting up on Mr Hooper's shoulder.

Ting-ting. Mr Hooper rang his little round truck's bell, for already it was an exhilarating and marvellous morning.

Friends made of colour, hummed The Cat with the Coloured Tail before stopping abruptly.

Again, a shadowy feeling had arrived. Then came words to a song he didn't want to sing.

> *Heart of the world,*
> *Dying in the night,*
> *Heart of the world,*
> *Stricken with blight.*

For a moment, he didn't know which way to direct the truck. Then he felt Mr Hooper's hand. Now Mr Hooper was giving him a reassuring and lovely neck scratch, the cat could finish his friendship tune.

Friends of all colours,
Friends made of light,
Make your heart lift,
Like a swallow in flight.

3

FOR A WHILE, THE moon-cream truck
trundled along from town to town.
Because this was the last day before their
holiday started, the moon-creams were extra
fantastic. If anyone was totally happy and
therefore bought a normal moon-cream, eating
it was just like licking sweet silver.

What a day they were having. Had there ever
been a Sunday afternoon so full of variety?

Heart Creams. Double Scoop Stars.

Hot Butterscotch Button Biscuit Sauce.

In the town before last,
Mr Hooper had even made
a moon-cream so like a lady
|ı. ı ılı ıIııı ıIıı ıılıI ııııı ıIıııI
worriedly thought it was going
to fly away before his first lick.

Or what about that one for the sad child
whose sea-loving dog had recently been run
over? A moon-cream so like waves lapping
that it had even been a little bit salty.

Greeny, Creamy,
Aquamariney.

When The Cat with the
Coloured Tail directed Mr Hooper
to a sad boy's house, a group of
children were standing up on a fence
being horrible.

"Fatty lumpkin," they were calling out. "Built like a pumpkin."

The Cat with the Coloured Tail pulled a face. Why would anyone bother to sing a mean song like that?

The bullying song grew even louder.

"Fatty, fatty lumpkin, face like a rotten pumpkin. Lumpkin pumpkin. Lumpkin pumpkin." As soon as Mr Hooper's truck came to a stop, the mean children took off down the street yelling.

The Cat with the Coloured Tail found the sad fat boy hiding under a bush in the front garden.

Lick, lick, lick. He began his work.
In a song that the boy could only hear as
purring, the cat began to sing.

Moon-creams as see-through,
As slender as air,
sang The Cat with the Coloured Tail.
A moon-cream is best,
For treating despair.

With astonishment all over
his face, the boy saw the cat's tail
turning as transparent as glass.
Let me see, thought Mr Hooper,
relishing the challenge, for not even
No Colour At All was too tricky
for him. The boy blew his nose,
watching as Mr Hooper made him
his special moon-cream. Again he

could hardly believe his eyes. Kindly, Mr Hooper had made him a see-through moon-cream that only The Cat with the Coloured Tail knew how to describe with a song.

Shimmering moon-creams,
All airy and bright, sang the cat.
This big boy can run now,
He's raced out of sight!

Mr Hooper and The Cat with the Coloured Tail looked at each other and smiled. They knew that for the rest of his life, the boy would remember the wonder of this afternoon.

So why was the dreary song about the awful black heart returning to the cat? He looked around quickly. Could Mr Hooper hear it too?

The Cat with the Coloured Tail shook his head as if he'd somehow got grass seeds in his ears.

Go away, he sang to the image of the black heart. After ringing the bell, he leaped straight into Mr Hooper's lap for comfort. It was beginning to occur to him that somehow the very heart of the world was sickened and sad.

Could he and Mr Hooper ever fix that?

He snuggled deeper before climbing right inside Mr Hooper's jumper. Now he felt better. Then, with his head poked out at the top, his ears suddenly pricked to the feeling of someone sad quite close by.

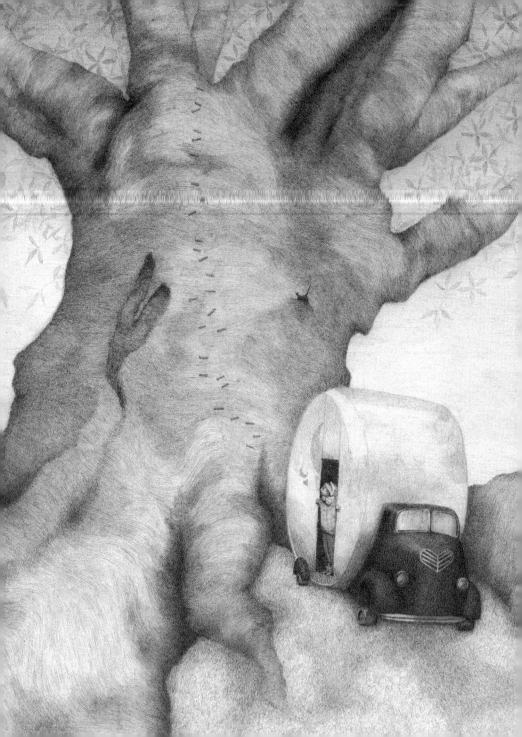

M R HOOPER, FOLLOWING HIS cat's directions, pulled up next alongside a beautiful old tree. With delight, he watched his cat rush up the trunk before disappearing along the branches. The Cat with the Coloured Tail loved climbing trees, but usually only got the chance if they'd stopped for a game of Spot the Heart.

Who is The Cat with the Coloured Tail going to find up there? wondered Mr Hooper. He bustled about at his truck's counter, checking

his ingredients, as well as selling a couple of
ordinary moon-creams to happy people.

The Cat with the Coloured Tail was about
halfway up the tree when he saw a pair of twin
sisters. They were sitting in their tree house,
each on a separate bed but both crying their
eyes out.

Little friends, let me tell you,
This is no dream, sang the cat, feeling his
whiskers begin to tremble.
It's a sign you need,
A Hooper's moon-cream.

Even at the unexpected sight of a tiny cat
with friendly whiskers, the sisters couldn't stop
crying. Their mother had never come home
from the hospital. Their mother had died.

Whose tears should he attend to first? The
Cat with the Coloured Tail looked from one
girl to the other. He began a song that the
sisters could only hear as the warmest purr.

"Puss, puss, puss," they crooned.

"Remember Mum at firecracker night?"
they said as one.

"She got a bit scared."

"Just a little bit. Really sparklers
were her favourite."

"Drawing words in the sky."

"Love hearts with our names inside."

Uh-oh, thought The Cat with the Coloured
Tail, suddenly realising from the feeling in
his whiskers what the sisters' favourite colour
involved. Firecrackers.

Gradually, the girls' sadness grew less, then
right before their very eyes, the cat's tail began
to light up.

My goodness, wondered
Mr Hooper at the sound of
many little snaps and loud
pops coming from the tree.
Whatever could be
going on up there?

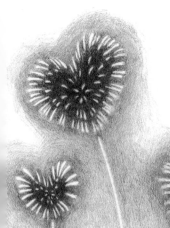

Only as his cat came whizzing down the trunk, closely followed by the girls, did the noises make sense.

Aha, thought Mr Hooper with delight wreathing his cheeks. A firecracker moon-cream? Could that be right?

> *Double-up, double-up,*
> *Firecracker creams,*
> sang the cat.
> *For girls who share everything,*
> *Every memory,*
> *every Mummy dream.*

Mr Hooper got going. In no time at all, a pair of triple-decker moon-creams were fizzing in his hands, in colours of every kind. Handing the moon-creams down to the sisters, and glancing over to his cat, Mr Hooper knew his firecracker moon-creams were an unmistakeable triumph.

The twins shouted out with excitement,
because they could imagine their mother
laughing too.

Together, Mr Hooper and The Cat with the
Coloured Tail watched the happiness of
the sisters. Together, they felt very proud.
They knew that for the rest of their lives,
whenever sad times came, the girls
would be comforted by the
memory of moon-creams
in celebration of their
mother's happiness on
firecracker nights.

As on any Sunday, the cat's favourite
moment arrived when he noticed
that the first evening star had
appeared in the sky.

Many people call it the Dog
Star but Mr Hooper and The
Cat with the Coloured Tail
always called it the Cat Star.

Tomorrow days are camping days,
sang the cat, thinking of their holiday
at the beach soon to begin the next day.

His eyes became brighter. He loved that at
this time of year Mr Hooper pulled on so many
beanies that he looked like a Super-duper
Triple Five Scooper. He loved that by the
time they left the town it was dark enough to
turn on the van's lights. Now the moon-cream
truck felt just as if it had been decorated for
Christmas.

When the image of the black heart of the world tried to swim again into The Cat with the Coloured Tail's mind, he flicked it away as if it were no more than a little lizard on a warm footpath.

He and Mr Hooper had worked hard today. Time for a lovely nap, if not in Mr Hooper's lap, then in his own special bed that Mr Hooper had made as a secret surprise for his birthday. The Cat with the Coloured Tail looked over to Mr Hooper.

"Of course," said Mr Hooper without needing to be asked. "You have a lovely catnap," he smiled, "while I find us a good spot to stay for the night. Then in the morning we'll drive to the sea."

Although made of a very old-fashioned biscuit tin, Mr Hooper had lined The Cat with the Coloured Tail's birthday bed with a soft

and tiny rug made up of all the colours of the rainbow. Mr Hooper had knitted it himself using bits and pieces of favourite old jumpers.

The moment The Cat with the Coloured Tail was deeply asleep, an awful dream snapped him awake. The heart of the world had grown shrunken and black. The heart of the world was in such trouble there clearly wasn't a second to lose.

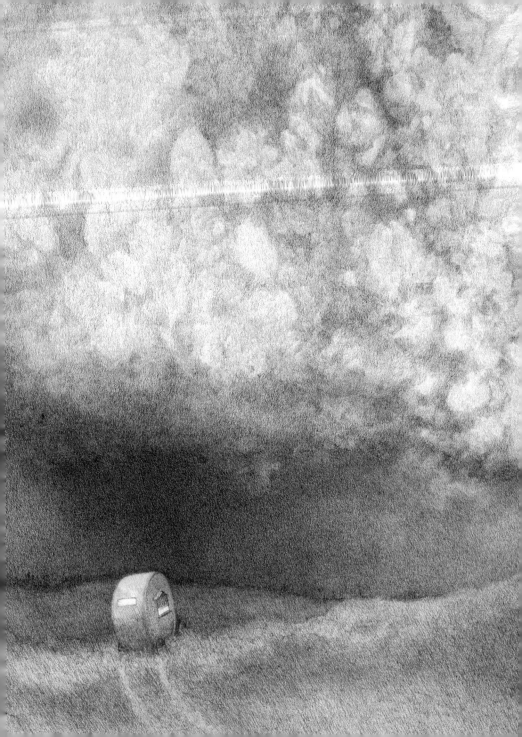

JUST AS THE CAT with the Coloured Tail realised the heart of the world was in danger, the storm that had been brewing all day finally burst over the moon-cream van. A rattle of hailstones obliterated the sight of any remaining stars. In fright, the cat leaped from his bed to sit next to Mr Hooper.

Then left, right, left-left, right, pointed his tail. Left, right, left-left, right.

Nothing like this had ever happened before. Mr Hooper felt as if his cat were moving them to

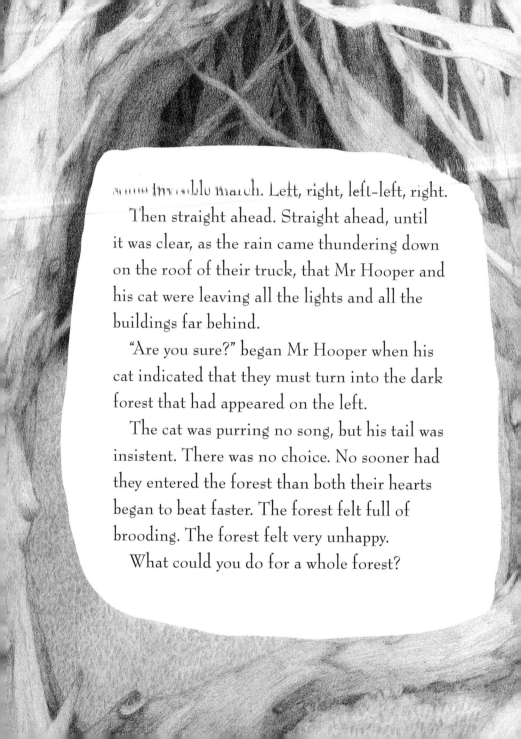

...... invisible march. Left, right, left-left, right.
Then straight ahead. Straight ahead, until
it was clear, as the rain came thundering down
on the roof of their truck, that Mr Hooper and
his cat were leaving all the lights and all the
buildings far behind.

"Are you sure?" began Mr Hooper when his
cat indicated that they must turn into the dark
forest that had appeared on the left.

The cat was purring no song, but his tail was
insistent. There was no choice. No sooner had
they entered the forest than both their hearts
began to beat faster. The forest felt full of
brooding. The forest felt very unhappy.

What could you do for a whole forest?

Mr Hooper stopped his ice-cream truck in order to see if there was a map somewhere. But there was, as ever, only one map and that was his cat's tail.

Then, to Mr Hooper's horror, in the light of the van, he saw something never seen before. He saw that, little bit by little bit, his cat's tail had begun to turn black. Not indigo blue. Not dusty black, such as a heart stone often sighted on any footpath of any town. Not glossy and black in the way of a heart spotted on the shiny coat of a dog. Not black like a whimsical flower shadow. But a sad deep black. A black such as a night that has never known stars. A black more dense than the forest all around.

Although Mr Hooper's cat's tail usually changed colour fast, right now it was changing hair by hair, as if tiny ants were filling it up.

As the road grew steeper, the cat moved even closer to Mr Hooper. Mr Hooper felt the cat paw in his hand begin to sweat with fear.

The road grew steeper.

Down, down the track was going. Every minute felt more dangerous. Down, down, down they were heading. If he could, Mr Hooper would have turned around. But there was never a chance. Down, down until it felt as if, at any moment, they might fall completely off the road.

When they did reach the bottom of the road, Mr Hooper switched off the engine but kept the headlights on. From the forest drifted a sad and lonely smell. The cat could feel an unknown terror coming into his tail and his whiskers.

Instead of jumping eagerly out of the truck window, as he had done for all of his life, The Cat with the Coloured Tail waited for Mr Hooper to open the door. Then into the deadly silence he gave a small miaow, which was a sure sign that something was very wrong.

Mr Hooper found his torch and shone it into the darkness. His cat had set off and was already quite far ahead in the beam of light.

They seemed to be making for a deep hollow. Mr Hooper's mood sank even lower.

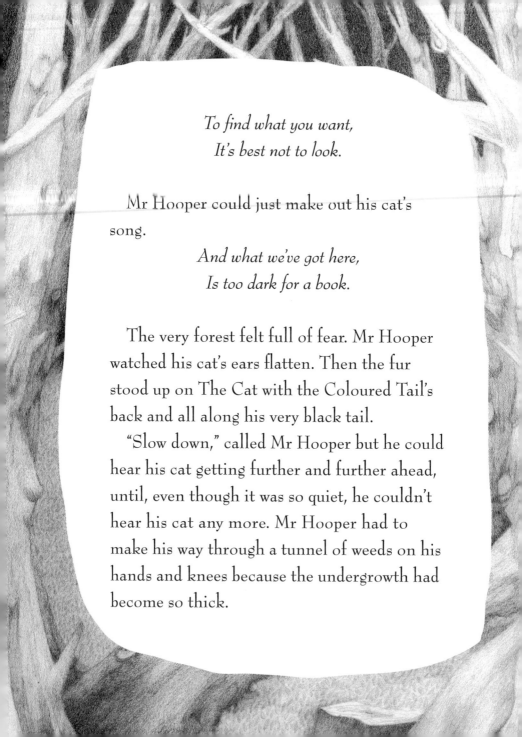

To find what you want,
It's best not to look.

Mr Hooper could just make out his cat's
song.

And what we've got here,
Is too dark for a book.

The very forest felt full of fear. Mr Hooper
watched his cat's ears flatten. Then the fur
stood up on The Cat with the Coloured Tail's
back and all along his very black tail.

"Slow down," called Mr Hooper but he could
hear his cat getting further and further ahead,
until, even though it was so quiet, he couldn't
hear his cat any more. Mr Hooper had to
make his way through a tunnel of weeds on his
hands and knees because the undergrowth had
become so thick.

Mr Hooper's knees hurt. He tried to speed up but it was no good. By the time he came out of the tunnel, he felt as alone as before The Cat with the Coloured Tail had come into his life. He felt that something terrible had happened to his cat and that they would never see each other again.

Mr Hooper had emerged at a creek. He spent a moment piecing together a broken sign. "Silent Creek" he read.

"To find what you want, it's best not to look," Mr Hooper tried singing, but it was no good, he just had to search for his cat. First, he went along the creek, heading east. Then he walked west. But true to the song, it was only after he'd totally given up that there! – there was his cat – sitting in a tree, studying something in the water. The Cat with the Coloured Tail, his tail pitch-black, pulled a face, licking sap out of his paws.

What was it that his cat had found?

Certainly not fish. What on earth? A heart, only just floating? Surely, that's what it was? A very small, very sad, very black heart.

In deep darkened water,
You're never alone, he heard his cat sing.
Shade of a tree,
And heart like a stone.

"Can you reach it without having to go in?" asked Mr Hooper.

A feeling of panic nearly overcame the cat. He crossed his whiskers.

"Be brave." Before Mr Hooper could offer any more suggestions, *sploosh*! His cat, who hated water, was in and swimming.

When The Cat with the Coloured Tail reached the barely floating heart, it was so sick and black that he felt afraid. Still, as a mother cat takes a kitten, he took it into his mouth, picking it up expertly, as if by the scruff of its neck.

Quickly, he swam to the creek's edge and scrambled up the bank out of the water.

Once on solid ground, something was clearly wrong with The Cat with the Coloured Tail's walking. He was weaving and staggering, his wet tail as thin as a whip. Mr Hooper, watching, thought that the heart in his cat's mouth must be very heavy.

No sooner had the cat reached Mr Hooper's side, than he dropped the heart. Now, his mouth opened as if he'd tasted something terrible. Now, he made a noise like crying. What was he trying to sing? Then the cat, whose tail was still as inky black as the night, lay down as if the effort had killed him.

"Oh no. Oh no? Please?" Mr Hooper put his hand onto his cat. "Oh no, no, please?" repeated Mr Hooper. He took his cat up into his arms but the cat stayed limp and lifeless. "Why, why?" called out Mr Hooper, but the forest remained quiet.

From the heart, rose a smell all bitter and black. Mr Hooper didn't just want to fling it back in the water, he wanted to crush the heart.

Instead, he crouched down to study the damaged heart more closely. It was so crooked it was in danger of turning into a shape no one could ever recognise as a heart again.

Gently, he laid his cat on the ground. Tenderly, he covered him with his shawl.

Then he took his handkerchief and put it over the heart that had killed his cat.

A tear glided down Mr Hooper's left cheek. Then down his right. Grief and despair came to Mr Hooper as he remembered all over again The Cat with the Coloured Tail's first arrival as a kitten. Back when Mr Hooper was so lonely he'd wished he were dead.

At the memory of the tiny kitten, Mr Hooper really began to weep. The bitter-smelling heart also seemed to ooze sadness.

Mr Hooper rested his hand on his cat's face. "No more heart finding without you," he murmured. "Without you, no more helping sad people to be happy." In utmost sorrow, Mr Hooper knew they'd never make a special moon-cream together again. Without his cat, how would he ever know what colours, what patterns to use?

As of now, every moon-cream would be darker than licorice. Tasteless like an old black stump.

Mr Hooper put his face close to his cat's ears to make a favourite secret noise, as if that might bring him back.

Nothing. No sign of life. Mr Hooper tried scratching behind his cat's ear. However, The Cat with the Coloured Tail's coat was so cold and wet it wouldn't feel nice for him at all. Mr Hooper realised that of course what they needed right now was a little camp fire.

Luckily, under his beanies, Mr Hooper always carried matches. Paper, leaves and a few dry twigs. A little camp fire, yes - that's it! Mr Hooper began to gather more dry leaves and twigs. Then he found some bigger branches as well as hauling over some of the broken "Silent Creek" sign. Next, a few good dry old roots.

Staring into the warm flames, careful that his cat's coat didn't scorch, Mr Hooper began to sing. He found that he was singing his cat's red and yellow song.

> *You can never be lonely,*
> *Out in the world,*
> *When your best reds and yellows,*
> *Are starting to curl.*

At the sound of the words, the fire crackled all the more merrily. As Mr Hooper sang, he ran one finger along the long, almost dry, once magical tail of his cat.

The camp fire coals glowed even redder. The flames were very yellow. Hearts made of ash and bark formed and fell apart.

The cat's tail began to tremble. His whiskers shook. Then he sneezed, got up and having industriously licked the top of Mr Hooper's hand, set to work cleaning his own face with his paw.

When he felt all lovely and clean, he started to chase the tail of happiness, the forest leaves under his paws making a sound like little biscuits snapping. The Cat with the Coloured Tail was spinning and leaping so much that Mr Hooper began to dance too. Then The Cat with the Coloured Tail began to lick the heart as if licking any sad person's cheeks.

6

M R HOOPER, HIS CAT riding on his shoulder, carried the heart back to the truck.

"I think what we'll have to do is take it with us to the sea," said Mr Hooper at exactly the instant his cat had had the same thought. What better remedy for any ill than salt water and the cry of the wild sea and its birds? "That is if we can get out of here. Maybe purr? If a song won't come?" Mr Hooper suggested. "Yes, you purr, as I drive. Remember how much your purring makes everybody feel special?"

At first, the cat whose tail was almost all still pitch-black could barely raise the stutter of a purr. Bravely, he kept trying.

Mr Hooper was also doing his version of a purr. Even the ice-cream truck's engine had a purring quality, taking them safely up to the top of the forest. But because purring's so hard for a human or an ice-cream truck to maintain for any length of time, soon it was just the cat.

Heart of the blackness, the cat sang a new line.
Heart of the night.
When we're down by the sea,
You'll be shiny and bright.

"That's it," encouraged Mr Hooper. "Down by the sea, you'll be shiny and bright."

The more the cat purred, the better they felt, the more smoothly the moon-cream van spun along on its button wheels.

"Black heart so dreamy," hummed Mr Hooper.

Moon-creams so creamy, joined in the cat whose tail, like the heart, was beginning to fill with the colours and shapes of tiny stars.

> *Creamier, creamier, creamier CREAMY!*
> *Landlocked heart that's been so sick.*
> *Maybe you need another lick!*

And as if the heart were someone still just a little bit sad, the cat once again went to work. The heart's bitter smell was changing. Now it held the fragrance of the earth after rain. And wasn't there also the lovely tang of eucalyptus leaves?

> *Look, Mr Hooper, Just look at that.*
> *The heart that we found,*
> *Is losing its black*, sang the cat.

For as they came within the sound of
the waves, a rosy tinge, like the sun coming
through clouds on the horizon, was creeping
across the heart. At the same moment, a line of
pink also began to move, like the first thread
of sunrise, through the middle of the cat's tail.

"But the heart will need some kind of boat,
don't you think?" said Mr Hooper as both the
heart and his cat's tail spangled like the sun on
the ocean.

He watched as his cat carried the heart and
carefully placed it into his own special biscuit
tin.

"Are you sure?" exclaimed Mr Hooper. "Your
own bed?"

The cat looked very pleased.

"Well," said Mr Hooper, "it is exactly the
right size. Want to stay in the truck?" Because
cats are usually worried by the waves of the sea.

But not The Cat with the Coloured Tail.

By the time Mr Hooper and his cat had reached the water, no one would ever have known that the heart of the world had once been sick. With one of Mr Hooper's red and yellow flag twigs at the front of the biscuit tin bed, the heart of the world was ready for the outgoing tide. In the shallows, Mr Hooper's feet began a new dance.

"Goodbye! Good luck!" said Mr Hooper,
raising his hand in farewell.

Goodbye! Good luck!
And stay in good health,
sang the cat as they watched the heart until it
seemed to be rising up to merge with the sun.

A smile as glorious as the rainbow on the
horizon spread over Mr Hooper's face. As
The Cat with the Coloured Tail tapped at
some sea foam with a paw, Mr Hooper saw
that for just a little time his cat's tail looked
as if it were a part of the rainbow itself.

"Now something special for breakfast," said Mr Hooper. Using all his skill, he began to compose two celebration moon creams. Mr Hooper's was big. The bottom scoop was bright red, the top one as golden as the sun.

The moon-cream he made for his cat was perfectly round, as if a little full moon in miniature had risen to the top of the cone. Was it the flavour of glimmery stars or was it tiny sardines?

The cat wasn't telling.

As they licked, a dreaminess was coming upon them.

Out on the ocean, imagined The Cat with the Coloured Tail, the heart of the world would by now be glowing gold. Yawning wisely, he nestled so close to Mr Hooper's face that Mr Hooper let out a lovely yawn too.

Just before sleep overtook them, The Cat
with the Coloured Tail sang a new song.

Heart of the world,
Out sailing the sea,
Remember us, please,
Mr Hooper and me.

THANKS

I began to write this story while camped on Ngarkat Country in the South Australian mallee. I finished it a few weeks later on Tjowilla Country on the floodplains next to a tributary of the River Murray. After that, many people from many places assisted the story on the long road to publication.

My eternal thanks to Tara Emma and Mark Kruszinski, Bodhi Mears, Ari Mears Lynch, Bella Lynch and Astrid Watt. Alice, Blake and Fletcher Barns, Bennett Mitchelhill, Bryan Carmen, Louis Page, Yvonne Mears, Barnaby Giles, Tanya Ellem, Cate Ellis, Bruce Long, Peter Ingenillem, Dave Funnel, Juliette Murphy, Jasper Dunne, Larissa Cooper, Katz Cowley. Clare Mahon, Claire Aman, Sharon Jones, Anjali Yardi, Kate Herd, Margaret Knight, Edna D'Arney, Tracey Price, Isla and Djuna Watchman-Naher, Herbert Tout and the late filmmaker Phillip Hearnshaw, Barbara Mobbs, Erica Wagner, Isabel. Ruby and Roy Bowling, Sheila and Peter Mears, Sarah Foster, Gaby Naher – you will remember what for.

To the Benevolent Fund of the Australian Society of Authors, particular thanks for once again keeping the wolf from my door.

At Walker Books I have appreciated working with my superb editors Nicola Robinson and Sue Whiting. The gifted labours of designer Gayna Murphy have not gone unnoticed.

Also a dip of my storytelling lid to my Giles boy nephew trio, "Hambone, Bluey and BB". Thank you for believing in Itchy, over in the dragon tree, all those years ago. Thank you for listening and for eating

76

what must have surely been the first moon-creams, freezing cold from the moon itself or so they seemed through your imaginative eyes. Thanks most of all to BB Barnaby, for believing so deeply in Itchy Hooper that you really thought he'd visited one night. Special thanks to Ari for often singing the moon-creams songs and to Bodhi for often drawing them.

Great gratitude to my book's midwives, Karin and Sonya, whose faith in the story never wavered and who found me a multitude of heart stones to pave the way towards publication. Without your unerring, poetical eyes, there'd be no cat star, cat stone and no many a magical thing besides. I particularly loved sharing the tick tack of words with you, Karin, and know that it's no coincidence you gave me my first thesaurus, the beauty of which ripples even now through all our memories of Mum and through all of my writing days.

Clarence River poet Geoff Page significantly improved the songs the cat sings.

As I wrote, four actual cats provided me with boundless inspiration and affection, beginning with the late silver korat, BelCanto, then the late lovely silver street cat, Ippy, who chased BelCanto away, followed by the blue Burmese, Milparinka (MILPIE) and the unexpected gift of a seal point Siamese kitten, PAUL Gallico.

Finally, when all is said and done, it's worth remembering that it was Vinita Laidlaw's handmade memoir of Ippy that first inspired me to try writing a cat book of my own. I thoroughly recommend the experience to everyone, no matter what your colour, race or creed. The world would be a far lovelier place if people lay down their anger and their guns to pick up their coloured pencils of childhood instead, to colour in my cat's tail if not their own.